Lonely Lost Falls

W9-CKL-241

Enchanted Forest

Campfire Cove

Crystal
Clear
Pond

Published in Nashville, Tennessee, by Thomas Nelson, Inc.,
Publishers, and distributed in Canada by Word Communications,
Ltd., Richmond, British Columbia.

ISBN 0-7852-8108-8

Printed in the United States of America

1 2 3 4 5 6 — 99 98 97 96 95 94

The Great White Buffalo Adventure

Carrie & Renee Minirth
with their dad, Buffalo Frank

as told to Christine Harder Tangvald

Illustrated by
Jim Conway

A JANET THOMA BOOK

THOMAS NELSON PUBLISHERS
Nashville • Atlanta • London • Vancouver

All the campers at Big Creek Ranch hurried to sit around the crackling fire at Campfire Cove. Each night they sang songs and waited for their special friend Buffalo Frank to tell a tale of long ago.

"Buffalo Frank, will you tell us another story about Big Creek Ranch?" asked one of the boys. "We brought you this smooth, smooth stone from Crystal Clear Pond."

"Why, thank you," said Buffalo Frank in his deep rumbly tumbly voice. "This is a mighty beautiful stone." His blue eyes twinkled and he smiled a big smile through his thick white beard.

"Buffalo Frank, is there a story about Crystal Clear Pond?"

"You bet! And a scary story it is!"

"Please tell us!" said all the boys.

"Oh, yes! Please, tell us!" said all the girls as they scooted closer and closer together.

Buffalo Frank held the smooth, smooth stone in the palm of his hand. "Hmmm," he said as he rubbed his thick white beard. "Now I remember. That's exactly where it happened. Right there at Crystal Clear Pond."

"Where what happened?" asked the children.

"Why the Great White Buffalo Adventure!" said Buffalo Frank.

"Really?" exclaimed the children. "Oh, Buffalo Frank, what happened? Please, tell us."

Buffalo Frank turned the smooth, smooth stone over and over in his fingers. He sat down close to the fire and began to tell this story:

Long, long ago, deep, deep in the wild, wild woods,
lived a happy pioneer family:
Father and Mother and their five girls—
Rachel, Renee, Carrie, Alicia, and Little Liz.

On a cold dark night—just like this one—
the family was camping down by Crystal Clear Pond.
"I think this is the very spot," said Father. "I think
my great-grandfather found that wounded white buffalo
right here—by Crystal Clear Pond."
"Buffalo aren't white!" said Carrie.

"Yeah, there's no such thing as a white buffalo," said Renee as the girls helped Mother sort a batch of wild blueberries.

Father leaned back and took a long swig of hot sassafras tea.

"Great-grandpa was amazed too," he admitted. "He had never seen a white buffalo before. But he nursed that calf back to health and turned him loose. No one has ever seen a white buffalo since."

"Well, I don't believe it!" said Carrie.

"Neither do I," said Renee.

"I do," said Alicia. "I believe you, Father."

The cozy campfire sent sizzling sparks spinning up into the black night.

"I'm sure glad we have this fire," said Rachel. "It is dark out there—really, really dark."

Suddenly the night air was shattered by a terrible sound. Screech! Screech! A scream so terrifying, the whole family sprang to their feet.

"What is that?" cried Carrie.

"Ssshhh!" commanded Father. "I think…it's…a panther!"

11

Out in the shadows something moved. Then it moved again. Screech! Screech! The panther screamed again—closer this time.

Father grabbed a big heavy stick of ironwood to use as a club, and he drew his knife.

Just then two eyes appeared in the darkness . . . two big yellow eyes!

"What will we do?" cried all the girls together.

"Move in close to the fire," said Father, "and stir it up. Big cats don't like fire. Maybe it will go away."

As the panther circled, the family could hear its low growl. Grrrr—Grrrr—Grrr.

Crackle . . . crackle . . . POP! Huge sparks shot out of the flames, lighting up the sky. Through the flames the family watched the powerful cat leap onto a ledge just above the campfire.

The panther's yellow eyes came closer . . .
and closer . . .
and closer.

"Oh, Father! What are we going to do?" cried Alicia.

"Don't panic," said Father as he gripped his knife and raised his ironwood club. "Keep the fire between you and the cat."

The panther crouched…ready to spring!
Father stood poised…ready to fight!
And then…
silence.

Not a sound…as they waited…
and waited…
and waited.

Suddenly the family heard a new sound.
Rumble, rumble, rumble!
The panther heard it too, and it froze like a statue.

Rumble, rumble, rumble!
The ground began to shiver.
The ground began to shake.
The ground began to quiver.
The ground began to quake.

The family could just make out the form
of a huge beast . . . a huge white beast
charging toward them.

It came thrashing and crashing across
the valley.

18

Rumble, rumble, rumble!

"It's a buffalo!" shouted Carrie. "A great white buffalo!"

Faster and faster it came.
Its eyes blazed.
Its nostrils swelled.
It puffed and snorted as it ran.

"Oh, no!" cried Carrie. "We're in double trouble
now! What will we do?"
"Get back! Get back!" commanded Father.
The huge white buffalo thundered right
past the huddled family, throwing chunks
of dirt high into the air
with every powerful
stride.

It lowered its head and charged straight at the crouching panther.

Screech! Screech!

Rumble, rumble, rumble!

The big black panther knew it was licked. In an instant it turned, and in one giant leap it was on the ground. It raced toward the safety of the forest—chased all the way by the angry white buffalo.

"Hooray, hooray," shouted all the girls.
"Hooray for the Great White Buffalo!"

The huge white beast turned to face the family. It pawed the ground with its giant hooves. It threw its head high into the air as a sign of triumph. Then with one loud snort it whirled again and galloped into the darkness of the night.

26

Rumble, rumble, rumble!

"Hey, Carrie!" said Renee. "Do you believe in the Great White Buffalo now?"

"Do I ever! I will never doubt it again—never ever!"

"Wow, that was a great story, Buffalo Frank," said all the children around the campfire. "But is it true? Was there really a great white buffalo?"

"Well, that's what some folks say," said Buffalo Frank as

he stroked his thick white beard. "In fact, that's why I'm called Buffalo Frank. My grandpa was called Buffalo Frank, and my dad passed the name down to me."

Then his face got very, very serious.
"You know, some folks say that

  —on a cold dark night,
  —when the big round moon shines so bright,
  —if you listen with all your might
you can still hear the thundering hooves of the
Great White Buffalo!"

 "Really?" whispered all the children.
 "That's what some folks say."

Long, long ago, deep, deep in the wild, wild woods,
lived a

HAPPY PIONEER FAMILY

Father   Mother   Rachel   Renee   Carrie   Alicia   Little Liz